What Do You Want That For?

Written by Alison Hawes

Illustrated by Lisa Smith

Dad and Callum went to a
flea market...

but Mom had to stay in the garden.
She had to shoo the birds away.

Shoo!

Callum bought an old soccer ball.

"What do you want that for?" asked Dad.

"It's for Mom," said Callum.

Callum bought an old wig.

"What do you want that for?" asked Dad.

"It's for Mom," said Callum.

Callum bought a hat and an old coat.
"What do you want those for?"
asked Dad.
"They're for Mom," said Callum.

Callum bought two old brooms.
"What do you want those for?"
asked Dad.
"They're for Mom, too," said Callum.

Callum bought an old pillow.

"What do you want that for?" asked Dad.

"It's for Mom," said Callum.

Callum and Dad went home.

"What do you want all those things for?" asked Mom.

"They're for you, Mom," said Callum.

"Thank you, Callum," said Mom.
"That's just what I want!"